IF I HAD A GRYPHON

Library of Congress Control Number: 2015931505

For Kallie, who knows exactly how
to handle a gryphon. – V. V.

Dedicated to all the unicorns out there.
You know who you are! – C. A.

Edited by
Samantha Swenson
The artwork in this book
was rendered in photoshop,
fairy dust and phoenix ash.

The text was set in Hank BT.
Printed and bound in China

Text copyright © 2016 by Vikki VanSickle
Illustration copyright © 2016 by Cale Atkinson

Library and archives Canada
cataloguing in publication
available upon request.

Published simultaneously in the United States of America
by Tundra Books of Northern New York, a division
of Random House of Canada Limited,
a Penguin Random House Company

Penguin
Random
House

TUNDRA BOOKS

Published in Canada by Tundra Books, a division of Random House of Canada Limited, a Penguin Random House Company

2   3   4   5   6   20   19   18   17   16

www.penguinrandomhouse.ca

GRYPHON

IF I HAD A

Vikki VanSickle

illustrated by
Cale Atkinson

Tundra Books

Last week I got a hamster.

My first and only pet.
He mostly eats and sleeps and hides
And gets his shavings wet.

If only I could have a pet
With strange, exotic powers,
I know that I'd find lots to do
To while away the hours.

If I had a unicorn,
I'd braid her silky mane.
I'd make her silver horseshoes
That tinkled in the rain.

We'd prance through fields of posies
And nibble nectarines.

I'd shine her horn with candy corn
To get a starry sheen.

Unicorns are pretty,
but they're also very shy.

On second thought,
I'd like to give a
hippogriff
a try.

A hippogriff needs lots to do,
Like RUN and JUMP and FETCH.
I'd take him to the dog park
To give his *wings* a stretch.

Though a hippogriff is tons of fun,
The dogs might find him scary.
And when it comes to playing ball,
Well, things could get quite hairy.

Perhaps I'll get a sasquatch
With burly, curly fur.

But she needs flying EVERY day,
Regardless of the weather.

If I had a kraken,

We'd swim and deep-sea dive,

But I would need a scuba suit

In order to survive.

If I had a dragon
With a temperamental SNOUT,
I'd need a fire extinguisher
to put her sneezes out.

Kirin needs a field of grass
At least an o c e a n wide.

Jackalope needs sturdy reins for bumpy, jumpy rides.

Phoenix needs a chimney nest
That's smoke and fire proof.

Manticore needs special floss
For EACH and EVERY tooth.

Harpies are too screechy;
Chupacabras like to bite.

Fairies play too many tricks
And kelpies hate the light.

Basilisk is slippery;
Chimera likes to scratch.

Mermaids brush
their hair all day

And sprites are hard to catch.

Perhaps a hamster's not so bad.
In fact, he's rather sweet.
I love his furry belly
And his teeny tiny feet.

He may not be a gryphon,
Or a creature from the sea,
But I am his and he is mine
And that's enough for me.